A girl not much taller than Mary
stood half in shadow,
half in the soft light.

From the candle in its pewter holder the flame shone upward on her delicate face, framed in dark braids. The pale light brightened her white lace collar, outlined the fitted bodice.

The gentle voice seemed actually to float upon the atmosphere as the girl glided backward, away from the cellar's gloom. ''I am Angelica Biondi.''

Mary felt as though she were standing before a mirror, talking to herself. She and Angelica Biondi looked alike!

''*Willkommen*,'' Angelica whispered. ''*Welcome, Maria.*''

Mary shivered. Her grandmother's name had been Maria Biondi.

THE SECRET ROOM DOWNSTAIRS

Ruth Willock

A MINSTREL® BOOK

PUBLISHED BY POCKET BOOKS

New York   London   Toronto   Sydney   Tokyo   Singapore

A MINSTREL PAPERBACK *ORIGINAL*

A Minstrel Book published by
POCKET BOOKS, a division of Simon & Schuster Inc.
1230 Avenue of the Americas, New York, NY 10020

ISBN: 0-671-72324-3

First Minstrel Books printing September 1992

10 9 8 7 6 5 4 3 2 1

A MINSTREL BOOK and colophon are registered trademarks
of Simon & Schuster Inc.

Printed in the U.S.A.

This book is written in loving memory of my mother, Mary Niklaus Willock, my grandmother, Louise Aeberhard Niklaus, both born in Winterthur, Switzerland, and my grandfather, Johann Baptist Niklaus, sculptor, born in Stilfs, the Austrian Tyrol.

I also dedicate this book to Peter Hovannes Turabian, whose devotion for so many years has been a loving memory for me.

R. W.
1992

THE SECRET ROOM DOWNSTAIRS

1

Through the Dark Archway

Mary raced across the square toward the row of old houses, clutching the iron key in her pocket. Something was going on over there, and she had to find out what those men and that huge tractor-derrick-crane thing were doing.

Just a minute ago Aunt Rosa had indicated the pink house through the dark archway and said, "That's where your grandmother lived when she was your age." Then she had turned away to look over the vegetables in the outdoor market.

Mary did not have time to waste on beans and carrots and eggs and April's daffodils. She had promised Grandma that if she ever got to Switzerland, she would visit that old house and look for the secret room.

Grandma had died last year in Boston.

Today, Mary's promise meant even more because of that. And she had the key in her hand and was wearing the old embroidered cap Grandma had given her. "They came from the house," Grandma had told her. "They belong there. You'll see, someday."

The moment Aunt Rosa had seen the cap on Mary, she had exclaimed, "So, *you've* got the cap! I was afraid it had been lost." She had tied the long ribbons under Mary's chin this morning before they'd left the house.

This was the first chance Mary Wood had had to see her grandmother's house since her mother and father had transferred her to Aunt Rosa's care at Zurich airport yesterday morning. That seemed ages ago.

And yet it was just last evening when Aunt Rosa had driven her to Wintertal in her little white car. She had insisted that Mary go to bed as soon as they'd arrived.

"Jet lag," she had told Mary. "You've come a long way from Boston—it must be four thousand miles—and there's a time change to get used to."

Mary had protested that it was too early and she was nearly eleven years old. But Aunt

Rosa—who looked and acted so much like Mother, same blue eyes, fair hair, and soft voice—had simply stated, "Plenty of time for you to explore. It'll be three or four days before your father completes his engineering assignment in Egypt."

Long before six o'clock this morning Mary was out of her bed, eager to get going. After unpacking Grandma's cap from its tissue, she had gone to the window to look down on the town.

Darkness was lifting from the valley, yet even at this early hour windows were lighted in all the houses, and bicycles and cars were moving along the roads.

She started to turn from the window when a blue blur on a bicycle streaked across the garden. Halfway along the path it halted abruptly.

It was a boy. Surprisingly, he waved in her direction before he sped off toward the gate and the hill road.

Aunt Rosa came up behind Mary and laid an arm across her shoulder. "That's my neighbor's son. You'll like him."

Mary had no time for boys. She was glad breakfast was ready so they could hurry down to the market Aunt Rosa had mentioned.

When they finally reached there, it seemed forever before Mary managed to get away alone.

And now something was definitely going on around the row of old houses where Grandma had lived when she was a little girl.

"Mary-y-y!" Aunt Rosa's voice echoed through the archway across the square behind her.

Mary stopped and turned beyond the cathedral, waiting for Aunt Rosa to catch up.

The pink house was just across the cobbles, beyond the narrow sidewalk.

Oh! It was beautiful, exactly as Grandma had described it. Mary loved it, even if the pink stone was crumbling a bit and the white paint on the shutters and windowsills was peeling.

Aunt Rosa came up beside her and set down her market bag. "It's really too bad," she said, looking up at the house.

"Too bad?" There *was* something ominous about this, Mary thought. All the houses in the row, and this one, looked empty and abandoned. And all that equipment down the road? She tugged at Aunt Rosa's sleeve. "Too bad?" she repeated.

Aunt Rosa nodded. "These houses are to be demolished."

"No!" Mary cried. "They can't be!"

Her aunt sighed. "We've tried," she said, as though she were talking to herself. "Many of us tried. But space is very important today. The Town Council—"

4

"Ask him," Mary interrupted, pulling her aunt toward a tall, serious-looking man in brownish coveralls. Papers and rulers and keys stuck out of his deep pockets, and bits of brick dust clung to his trousers.

"Aunt Rosa, *please* tell him I'd like to see Grandma's house. I'd like to see inside."

Mary would rather be alone when she explored, but apparently there was little time to waste.

Aunt Rosa called out in German, "Pardon me! Are you the supervisor here?"

The man nodded, frowning. *"Ja, Ja,* I've just been looking over the block. Got to plan the first move."

"I understand," Aunt Rosa said. Mary wished *she* did. But she listened carefully to the Swiss German as her aunt went on. "My niece and I wondered whether we could possibly get inside this house." She reached out and touched the pink stone with the tips of her fingers.

"Well . . ." The man hesitated, his gray eyes thoughtful. "This row is practically bolted up now. I'm not supposed to open the houses again."

"You do have the keys, don't you?" It was obvious that one of his pockets was lumpy with keys attached to an enormous ring.

5

"Naturally. But"—he pointed to the corner house—"that one is scheduled to go first. The outer door will be collected soon."

"Collected?" Mary's voice, a little squeaky, echoed her aunt's.

"*Ja, ja*. Antique dealers and the Wintertal museum have bought all the doors."

"Bought all the doors!" Mary could have cried right there.

Grandma's door was beautiful, even more elaborate than the others, its dark wood bolted with hammered iron, studded with glistening nailheads. The key panel was of iron, too, the keyhole as large as an acorn.

They were going to rip that off and sell it! She almost wanted to kick that supervisor.

And she certainly wasn't interested in his suggestion that they just look inside the corner house. "Except for a window or two," he told them, "they're all the same."

Mary was very happy to hear Aunt Rosa murmur, "Not quite. My mother lived in this pink house a long time ago."

Without another word the supervisor lifted out his keys. Mary watched, fascinated, as he selected one that looked exactly like her own.

And then, almost too quickly, they were on the stone step. His key clicked, the door groaned open.

6

After the brilliant daylight in the square Mary found it difficult to see for a moment. A flashlight miraculously appeared from another of the supervisor's pockets. Its circle of light moved over the flagstone floor. All Mary could see were streaked and stained walls spotted here and there with a lighter shape, which indicated where something had stood, a picture might have hung.

Mary lagged behind the man and her aunt. At every step her mind and her heart rebelled against a stranger here. It seemed to her that the house was actually against them; the damp, cold air enclosed them like wet wool.

Her aunt shivered. "It's so chilly in here," she said.

"Such old houses." The man grunted. "Never any central heating, of course." He stopped at a streaked wooden door. There was a metallic *clack* as he lifted a latch, and they peered over the threshold into a bleak, empty room.

Aunt Rosa backed away, drawing Mary with her. "Br-r-r . . ." She shuddered, fastening the top button of her coat. "The place wasn't very well kept, was it?" She turned toward the staircase leading to the upper floor. But Mary did not move.

She was watching the darting beam of the flashlight. Now it wavered over the balustrades

7

that curved up to the floor above. Then it descended and struck across the carvings on a low arched door that was deeply shadowed, all but hidden by the overhang of the stairs.

That door, Mary was certain, opened on the circular staircase that led to Grandma's room. She must get there somehow.

The supervisor slapped the walnut newel post with the flat of his hand. "Up there"—he pointed the torch—"same as down here. Empty and dirty. The last owner"—he shrugged—"a careless old man. He knew the building would come down."

He glanced at his watch. "Well, I'll have to lock up now. Must arrange the lunch hour for the men."

Mary was glad to get outside again even if the sun had disappeared, glad to finish with the thank-yous and the *adieux,* but she watched anxiously as the supervisor locked the outer door. The tips of her fingers touched the key in her pocket. She was so deep in thoughts and worries that she barely listened to Aunt Rosa.

"Disgraceful," her aunt murmured as they crossed the cathedral square.

"Imagine that ogre who bought the family's house permitting it to run down like that!"

At the end of the dark passage back to the

market square, Mary touched Aunt Rosa's arm. "After lunch, while you're at work at the museum," she pleaded, "may I come back and just look around these old streets?"

Aunt Rosa hesitated. "Are you sure you'll know the way home?"

"Oh, yes," Mary answered promptly. "I turn left at Tor Street over there where the road curves up the long hill."

Her aunt looked thoughtfully at Mary. "You won't bother that man, will you? He's very busy, you know."

"I won't bother him," Mary promised. She meant it. If anything, she hoped to avoid him.

2

Inside the Pink House
—Alone

After lunch in Aunt Rosa's cozy dining alcove, Mary and her aunt walked down the hill and parted at the marketplace. It was after two o'clock, and the square was empty now. She remembered that Aunt Rosa had told her that the farmers went home for their midday meal.

For a moment Mary felt very much alone. There was not one colorful stall, not one bright umbrella, not one shopper anywhere.

Her cold fingers reached down into her pocket and closed over the iron key. Now was the time to try to get into Grandma's house, to look for the secret room.

She hurried through the dark passageway into the cathedral square. How incredibly silent all of the old town's streets were, she thought as she plunged past the half-timbered exit of the arch. Silent and so empty.

And misty.

No.

It was snowing! Fine snow, not mist, blurred the outline of the twin spires of the cathedral, the chestnut trees, the iron railing. She could barely see the row of old houses beyond.

And it was so silent in the square that Mary looked over her shoulder, half wishing that someone would appear. Except for a single pigeon that strutted across the churchyard, she might have wandered into a town after a Pied Piper had lured everyone away. It was a little scary.

She drew her collar up around her. It certainly was cold for April.

Mary actually jumped when the church bell *bonged* the half hour after two. The sound hummed around her. She held tightly to the key in her pocket, for there was something comforting in just knowing it was there.

She walked around the ancient stone church toward the pastel houses that were doomed to destruction. It still made her angry to think that the Town Council—whoever they were—wanted to tear them down. She guessed she did not understand grown-ups sometimes. Just look at Grandma's house!

The only thing that was missing was the sign that Grandma said had once swung from its wrought-iron brace—or *was* it missing?

No. How had she not seen it before? For, now, there it was, a beautiful carved plaque tinted in many colors. From where she stood, it looked like a scene from the Bible. And below were carefully chiseled letters, which she spelled out, trying to recall what the word *Bildhauer* meant.

The man who had made that sign was an artist and educated. She remembered now. Father had explained that long ago, signs on very old houses and inns were usually just pictures because not everyone could read or write. The picture showed the profession or occupation of the householder.

She wondered whether the *Bildhauer* could have been Grandma's famous ancestor, and hers. And was that gleaming tinted sculpture a sample of his work?

Mary felt as though she had stepped into the world Grandma had talked about, the world of four centuries ago. She did not see or hear a bicycle, an automobile, a truck, or a crane. Even the silence was different.

And now, an odd sound. She was certain that she heard the sharp rhythmic beat of horses' hooves, the grate of metal wheels on stone. *Clop. Clop. Clop.* Louder and louder the sounds came. And whatever it was came toward her, faster and faster.

Mary leapt back just in time. Her heart thudded nearly as loudly as the horses' hooves. A yellow carriage like something she had seen only in a museum or in pictures loomed between her and the stone houses across the lane. The coachman flicked his whip over two fine gray horses!

A coach and horses? *Where had they come from?*

She peered through the snow as the yellow blur rocked past. Then, as quickly as they had appeared, carriage, horses, clatter, everything vanished.

Where had they gone?

It was minutes before she could move again, could concentrate on the pink house across the cobbled lane. And then what she saw when she squinted through the fine snowflakes made her heart thump again.

From one of the two chimneys on the pink house—it was the only house with two chimneys—a faint thread of smoke mingled with the veil of snow and drifted off over the rooftops.

13

Someone must live in Grandma's house! Mary's heart continued to pound. But where did they live? In the secret room?

She couldn't understand any of this. Maybe someone lived upstairs. Or downstairs. Maybe the Town Council had forgotten to notify them. She must warn them.

She started to run toward Grandma's house, the key clutched tightly in her hand. At the stone step she reached up, lifted the knocker, and when she dropped it, the door moved inward, away from her.

Mary caught her breath.

The supervisor had locked the door. She had watched him.

She drew the key from her pocket and looked down at it, remembering then what Grandma had said: *"I've often wondered whether just having the key in my hand hadn't opened the secret door for me."*

A chill wriggled up Mary's spine. She tried to call out, but only a peculiar croak came from her dry throat. She stared at the few inches of darkness between the door and its frame.

It was seconds before she dared touch the door again. And although her fingers barely grazed the wood, the old hinges creaked, and the door swung back. Except for a faint gleam at the end of the flagstone passage, there was no sign of life.

And yet the house smelled lived-in—and somehow familiar! It smelled of pine forests and Grandma's sort of cooking and warm baked bread, of all things!

But after the door swung shut behind her with rather a loud bang and she was swallowed by the shadows, it was as quiet as the street had been. Quieter, Mary thought. Too quiet.

Shakily she called out in her best Swiss German: "Is anyone there? Is anyone at home?" But only a hollow echo answered her.

She strained to adjust to the darkness. What was she afraid of? The place was supposed to be empty. Nevertheless, she tiptoed a little unsteadily past the wooden stairway that angled upward.

Her goal was the gleam beyond the arched door blocking the end of the corridor. And she knew now, even before she touched the iron latch, that it, too, would open without a key.

Beyond, there was the luminous glow just as Grandma had described. It highlighted a heavy ceiling beam of blackened timber so low that she could almost touch it. And the staircase was so narrow that she wondered how grown-ups could have used it.

Holding on to a heavy rope—Grandma had

mentioned the rope—she started down. The stone steps were pie-shaped wedges certainly not wide enough for grown-up feet unless they were put down sideways.

This must be the corkscrew staircase, the stairs Grandma had used! These must be the steps to the secret room!

At last! At last!

In her eagerness she slipped on a moldy step, scraped her knee against the rough wall, and sat down hard. Pain seared her leg, but she pushed herself up, anxious to see what lay ahead.

Without the light she would never have been able to follow these steps. As she hobbled on, she actually felt the welcome warmth. It was as though someone were lighting the way.

The cellar she stepped into was long and narrow; near the end was a woodbin stacked with logs. The light glanced off the rough bark, throwing the shadow of the woodpile toward her.

And the aroma! The hot bread! Spices. An elusive scent that reminded her of honey.

She leaned away from the bottom of the stairwell so that she could see past the woodbin. It was from a narrow slit in the wall that the light wavered.

Abruptly a door slammed shatteringly above her. Heavy footsteps clumped overhead.

"Who is there?" A man's voice shouted in Swiss German.

It was the supervisor!

Instantly the wavering light, the scents of bread and honey disappeared.

And Mary stood alone in total darkness.

3

The Iron Ball Strikes

She felt trapped and frightened. And ashamed. Entering a house without permission was bad enough, but explaining to that stranger was going to be very difficult.

And it was bitter cold now; her knees were shaking, her hands icy. Nervously she reached for the rope banister. But instead of a rope, her stiff fingers closed on a wooden rail.

A wooden rail! Where was the rope?

There was no time to wonder. For she heard a thump and a bump, a loud, *"Ach!* That ceiling beam!"* followed by a clatter of footsteps on the stairs.

18

Mary held her breath while a circle of light bobbed and jerked toward her.

In a second the light shone on the man's heavy brown shoes. In the next instant she was dazzled by the rays from the flashlight.

"What are *you* doing here, young one?" The supervisor's voice boomed.

Right then, in the chill, dank, abandoned cellar, Mary wondered, indeed, what she was doing there.

Her hand clenched the rail for support. "The— the door was open," she stammered at the shadowy figure.

"So? And do you always enter any open door?" The man's face was only a blur above her. "Eh? Is that the way you were brought up?"

"No, sir." Mary's chin came up, and she tried to look into the man's eyes. But all the shadows were the wrong way, reversed because the light was below his face. She stuttered, "You see, sir, I—I—came in because my grandmother—"

"I know, I know," he interrupted, waving his flashlight so that beams of light struck out in all directions. "But no one lives here now. You see that."

Mary touched the fabric of his sleeve. "There was smoke from the chimney, and—and wood in

19

the bin." She stopped. She decided not to mention the light. Perhaps she had said too much already.

"Wood in the bin, eh?" The supervisor strode past her.

She turned to watch as the rays from his flashlight shone full on the stone flooring behind her.

It was completely empty!

"Wood, eh?" The man chuckled. "Come along," he said, almost kindly now. "You must be seeing things, little one. Believe me, with the cost of wood today, no one would have left any behind."

He swung his flashlight back toward the stairs. Then his arm halted, and he raised the light over Mary's head.

"By the way, I meant to ask your aunt. Where did you get that cap you are wearing?"

"It was my grandmother's."

"*Nei, nei!* It would be much older than that," he said. "When I saw you with your aunt, you reminded me of a painting somewhere. The museum, maybe." Mary thought she heard a sigh before he went on. "Caps like that are from the time when young girls made all their own clothes, even wove the fabric."

He turned away and started up the stairs. "Sometimes I wonder if the world wasn't better off then."

20

Dazed, Mary followed silently. No wood in the bin, she was thinking, no guiding light? Had she been daydreaming after all?

The only thing that was the same was the ceiling beam at the top. She noticed especially because the man struck his head again and groaned.

Upstairs, Mary sniffed the closed-in air. No honey-scent or aroma of home-baked bread. The hall smelled the same as it had that morning, damp and moldy like a long-forgotten house.

When the man pulled back the heavy front door, sunlight dazzled her. Across the lane the daffodils stood tall and straight in the shadow of the rhododendrons. The garden was only thinly blanketed by the earlier snow.

The man yanked the door shut behind him and glanced down the lane toward the corner.

There, instead of the handsome yellow coach, the cobbled road was blocked by the ugly yellow crane Mary had seen that morning. An enormous ball suspended from a glistening cable. And that ball was aimed straight at the corner house four doors away.

The supervisor waved his arm in a signal.

Mary stood, horrified.

Iron crashed against stone. The top story of the house buckled. Almost like a slow-motion picture, stone, glass, windowframes, shutters, and part of the tile roof showered inward and to the street below.

Ready to pummel the man beside her, Mary cried, "They can't do that!" She glared up at him. "They've got to stop!"

But all he did was shake his head. "That's the way things go," he said. "Here today, gone tomorrow."

"Not tomorrow!" Mary nearly did cry. *"This house—my grandmother's house—can't be knocked down tomorrow!"*

"Ach, nei," he said. "One house at a time. It could be days before we get this far." He stepped down to the pavement and cocked his head to one side. *"Ja, ja,"*—Mary wondered why the Swiss so often said "yes" and "no" twice—and then he went on, "If it snows more it could take longer."

Mary watched him move away toward the workmen with their mechanical monster, which was already humming back into position.

How can I stop them? she was thinking. How can I prove that someone lives in this house behind us, that something is there?

She *had* seen the smoke from one of the chimneys. And the light at the bottom of the staircase, and the firewood. She had smelled the baking bread.

22

But only when she was alone. No one would believe her!

In fact, she had to prove to herself that someone did live here.

And why not? she thought. Why not prove it right now?

She started to move backward on the step, watching to see that the supervisor was completely occupied. Then she turned quickly and pushed hard against the heavy door that had clicked shut so firmly a minute ago.

This time she was not at all surprised to feel it move inward, away from her, silently and smoothly. It was almost as though someone had drawn it back from inside.

4

"Welcome, Maria"

The long corridor lay before her, dark and gloomy once more. But the instant her foot touched the stone floor again, the familiar lived-in aromas enfolded her.

Someone did live here. *She just knew it!*

And now she must hurry.

Without a sound she closed and double-latched the iron bolt, pausing long enough to press her ear against the cold wood. No, that man's heavy shoes were not clumping back over the sidewalk.

The house was very quiet. She could not even hear the clank of that awful machinery.

She clenched her fingers, her right hand still

holding tightly to the key in her pocket. With that reassurance she turned and ran toward the carved door at the end.

The same luminous glow lighted the pie-wedge stairs for her. The same heavy rope guided her down toward the warmth and the inviting scents.

She did not hesitate at the bottom, did not even glance at the woodbin. She was too eager to reach her goal—the door—the slit—the light—whatever it was that beckoned her on. Her feet seemed lighter, swifter, as she sped through the dark cellar.

Far at the end the narrow opening in the wall widened slowly. Mary pulled back and caught her breath.

Something moved. A flame lit up a gleaming door of carved and polished wood. Candlelight glowed on the figure that appeared.

A girl not much taller than Mary stood half in shadow, half in the soft light.

From the candle in its pewter holder the flame shone upward on her delicate face framed in dark braids. The pale light brightened her white lace collar, outlined the fitted bodice.

The gentle voice seemed actually to float upon the atmosphere as the girl glided backward, away from the cellar's gloom. "I am Angelica Biondi." Her gesture was almost a curtsy. The words that

25

followed were different: not German, not Latin. Did Angelica mean "Welcome"?

Mary could barely whisper, "Thank you." Her voice had almost deserted her.

She felt as though she were standing before a mirror, talking to herself. She and Angelica Biondi looked alike! Round face, hazel eyes, the same short nose, the same smile.

And yet the girl's speech was so different, her clothes like pictures in a book of old-time costumes Her long hair, slightly darker than Mary's, was braided and intertwined with silk ribbons of deep rose. The gray wool dress nearly touched the tip of the buckled shoes that made no sound at all on the stone floor.

The girl moved as lightly as the draft that blew the door shut behind them.

Inside the room she placed the candle holder on a shining trestle table. Murmuring something in the strange language, she lifted Mary's coat from her shoulders.

The coat was in Angelica Biondi's hands before Mary remembered the key. In haste she grasped at the pocket, plunged her hand into it, and drew out the key. She sighed with relief.

Both girls stared at the wrought-iron piece in Mary's hand, then looked up at each other.

Angelica traced its bow with a slender finger.

"Willkommen," she whispered. "Welcome, Maria."

Mary shivered. Her grandmother's name had been Maria Biondi.

She shook her head. "My grandmother was named Maria." Then she added, *"My* name is Mary. Mary Wood."

5

The Secret Room

Mary simply stared at Angelica, thinking, I'm here at last in Grandma's secret room; a room from another world, another century. And I am not alone!

"You have come a great distance." Angelica spoke softly. "You will be weary and must share my bread. Do be seated." With a scarcely audible swish of her long skirt the girl glided from the room through another doorway.

Mary leaned against the nearby table. She was not weary, she was just wavery.

"*. . . come a great distance . . .*"

Angelica's voice hovered in the silence while

28

Mary struggled to adjust to this other world. Across the Atlantic from Boston to Zurich to Wintertal. Thousands of miles, as Aunt Rosa had said. And how many years? How long ago had time stood still in this lovely room?

Yet, in spite of it all—the distance, the strangeness—Mary felt at home just as Grandma had when she had played here.

The girl's speech was only partly the Swiss dialect that Mary knew. But some of her words must be in the old language of the eastern valley that Grandma had once mentioned. The valley through which Anton Biondi had traveled on his way to Wintertal.

Biondi? Mary thought. Anton Biondi? The girl's name was Angelica Biondi!

As clearly as though her grandmother were in the room, Mary could hear her say, *"Anton created beautiful tiles,* as *iridescent and lustrous as pearls."*

Could he be Angelica's father?

Mary looked around her.

In the far corner, its thousand colors gleaming beneath the pearl-like radiance of its enamel, stood a magnificent tile stove. It was as tall as the room and so large around that if she and Angelica stretched their arms out, they could barely meet each other's hands.

Each tile was a separate painting touched with gold, ornamented with sculptured figures in ancient costumes. The stove was topped with a crown of golden porcelain that reached the beamed ceiling.

And beyond the stove itself, up two tile steps, Mary spied a seat of tiles built into its own tiled corner. Was that Grandma's favorite seat where she had found the cap—Mary's cap?

Mary started toward the magnetic warmth just as the door closed softly behind her.

She swung around.

"That cap you are wearing," Angelica murmured. "Where did it come from?" Bowls and a jug rattled a little as she set down her tray.

"My grandmother." Mary glanced back at the tile seat in the corner. She was not sure whether she should ask the question in her mind, but Angelica, nodding, broke the silence.

"Not long ago, when I was younger than you, I wove and embroidered one like that." She reached out to touch it.

Mary felt only the faintest stir of air above her head. No more. But she heard the whispered, "I am happy that it suits you so well."

Smiling, the girl turned to the table and drew up two carved stools. She held out a ceramic bowl filled with chunks of strange black bread and cakes. "Please," she said.

Selecting a crisp seedcake, Mary watched Angelica pour creamy milk from the jug, then looked toward the smaller door.

"Won't your mother be coming?" she asked. "Or anyone else?"

The two dark braids swung as Angelica shook her head. "My mother is no longer with us." A tear slipped down her cheek, then was lost in the lace of her collar. "But there was news of my father today. Only minutes before you came, the post coach brought his message."

The post coach? Mary's thoughts whirled back to the clatter of hooves, to the yellow coach in the lane outside.

"My father is on his way home, Mary! And when he comes"—Angelica's eyes were sparkling—"he will bring more of the proper clay from the riverbeds. Then he shall finish his work."

She moved soundlessly to the tile stove.

Mary noticed then that toward the wall one oblong square of tile, an area no larger than a school exercise book, was missing from the stove.

Angelica brushed the stove with the tips of her

fingers. "This will be his finest work," she said proudly. "You shall see."

"Oh, I hope it will be soon!" Mary tried not to think of the unmentionable beast chugging away down the lane, crushing houses into bits.

As though she understood, a shadow touched Angelica's eyes. "It must be soon. . . ." Her voice trailed off. "But surely you will come back, *please!*"

Mary dared not mention her fears. "Yes, yes," she said, "if I can."

"I shall wait for you." The girl seemed anxious, paler now, or was it because she faced a blaze of candles?

Something bothered Mary, something about the candlelight and the darkness. But there were so many new things to see and touch, and now there were new fragrances and tastes. Nutmeg-spiced milk and thick mountain honey. She wished she could save some of this delicious bread for Aunt Rosa.

Everything was different: the food, the pottery it was served on, the room.

It was almost spooky; shadowy, and the corners dark. The only light came from the honey-gold candles and the gleaming fire beneath the huge tile stove.

Suddenly she knew what puzzled her. There

were no windows! *That* must have been what Grandma had meant when she had said the room was different. *"Closed in by carved and paneled walls."*

When she could talk without her mouth full, she said, "Do you mind living by candlelight?"

"We do not *live* down here!" Angelica burst out. She glanced toward the ceiling, then to the smaller door. "My father's kilns—" She paused before she added, "We are not always here in these downstairs rooms."

Mary's mind whirled from kilns, which she knew were used in ceramic-making, to Angelica's bewildering half-finished statements. Not wanting to pry, she was uncertain what to say next.

She put down her beaker of milk. "But—but—" she stuttered, finally, "when you *are* down here, you'd never know whether it was snowing or not!"

Angelica laughed aloud. "Weather does not matter if one is happy!"

"Yes, it does, Angelica!" After she spoke, Mary wished she could take back the words. But it was too late.

Angelica said quickly, "Why do you speak of snow? It is spring now. The daffodils are blooming in the square."

"It was snowing when I came here."

Angelica's smile faded. "That will hinder my father's journey."

Mary wanted to say, "And it might stop that yellow monster," but she held her tongue this time. A new thought had struck her. The Town Council certainly could not demolish the house now. It could not bulldoze *people* away.

"Never mind," Mary murmured almost to herself. "I'll tell—"

"Not yet!" The girl's words were pleading, anxious. "Tell no one of our secret room, Mary. Promise me."

Mary felt trapped. Only snow and ice could delay the impending doom, then. And weather could not be trusted. Even in Boston anything could happen in April. It could snow one minute, then rain could wash it all away.

Oh, what shall I say? she wondered. What can I tell her?

"Promise!" Angelica repeated. "You must come again."

"I'll try. It may not be easy." Mary was thinking of Aunt Rosa and the supervisor and the huge yellow crane. She had another thought, then, though somehow she was not sure it was possible. "Could you come home with me?" she asked finally.

Angelica shook her head slowly. "I think not," she whispered. "I cannot cross the threshold into your time. . . ."

Mary drew a deep and shaky breath. She was not really surprised; she was worried. She did not want to lose her new friend.

"Mary!" Angelica's cool fingers touched hers. "*Please* stay awhile now. Come and see what we can do together!"

She drew Mary around the table to a beautiful doll's house, an exact replica of Grandma's pink house.

On her knees Mary peered into the top floor windows. Oh! What perfect doll-size four-poster beds and chairs and tiny chests! And when Angelica unhinged the peaked roof to let down the entire front panel, they could look straight into the front rooms. In every one Mary noticed a tiny tile stove built into a corner.

The house was simply fabulous, and the dolls looked like real people!

"This is like my father." Angelica leaned over and touched a handsome man doll whose sweeping mustache and black waving hair gave him the dashing air of a musketeer. He was seated at a trestle table, holding a quill pen smaller than a canary feather. The parchment beneath his hand was the size of a postage stamp.

Angelica touched the room above. Her voice
broke as she whispered, "This is . . . my mother."
Beneath silken coverlets in the four-poster bed,
a beautiful lady doll slept in frilly cap and long-
sleeved nightdress.

Perhaps because of the memories, Angelica did
not linger there. She pointed to a plump doll in
cap and full skirts standing over a tray in the
quaint kitchen.

Mary did not need words to tell her who that
was! The Grandma doll's dainty fingers hovered
over miniature pottery and pewter utensils.

Delighted, Mary leaned on her hand and stretched
around toward the rear of the doll's house, looking for Angelica. "Aren't *you* in any of the
rooms?" she asked.

When there was no answer, she glanced up at
Angelica.

Color flooded her new friend's face. "Not
yet." She seemed embarrassed. "I was wondering whether you might like to do that now,
Mary."

Mary touched Angelica's sleeve, which was
soft as gossamer and cool as new-fallen snow.
"I'd love to," she said.

Angelica moved to the table and opened a
carved box. From a mound of woolen, silk, and
flaxen remnants, she lifted two girl dolls, clad

36

only in white slips. "You see, it is *my* duty to dress the dolls." She held up one doll. "Perhaps we could dress this one in a costume such as you wear. That unusual blue frock, for instance."

Mary gazed down at her jumper and white pullover. *Unusual?* And yet, she thought, compared to Angelica's fitted bodice and long full skirt, she supposed her clothes were different.

Angelica watched Mary drift the oblongs and squares of silk brocades and stiff homespuns through her fingers. Only one piece of pearl-white silk seemed like a fabric her mother might buy today. How could they make a modern outfit out of any of this?

Suddenly she had an idea. The dolls were about as tall as half the length of a new pencil. A doll's jumper would not require much fabric.

She examined the hem of her blue jumper. Her mother believed in wide seams and deep hems "so they can be let out as you grow." There was plenty of the soft wool to make a little A-line jumper for this tiny doll.

Angelica protested at first, but finally she produced scissors, thread, needles, and silver thimbles. Together, they snipped, measured, shaped; then carefully they stitched Mary's uneven hemline back into position.

For the turtleneck pullover Angelica offered a

strip of soft white knit that looked as though it might once have been part of someone's winter underwear. They giggled when Mary mentioned that.

What a magical afternoon! Mary had always liked to sew, especially to create something out of almost nothing. But today was *special.*

Angelica's doll was perfect, of course. Its gray frock was a duplicate of hers, with the same apron and collar of gathered lace. The cap was very much like Mary's.

Minutes, maybe hours sped by. Mary did not think of time.

This was fun, and it was history. Wasn't it?

When they had finished, Angelica knelt at the front of the doll's house. But instead of the Angelica doll, she placed the doll in the blue jumper on the steps before the house, her hand on the miniature knocker.

Smiling, she wrapped the little sixteenth-century figure in a fold of silk smaller than a handkerchief and laid it in Mary's hand.

"This one is for you," she said.

6

Is It a Dream?

The doll lay light as a rose petal in Mary's palm. She stared down at it, thinking: This must all be a dream. Angelica, this old, old house, this lovely room. And now this tiny doll.

Is it a dream? she wondered.

She closed her eyes, half-afraid to open them again, but at that very instant she heard the fire crackle and spit across the room. Turning, she was certain she saw a burning log fall from the tray into the metal basin beneath. And there was Angelica, deftly raking the ashes, rolling another log onto the grate.

Beneath the stove's curved legs, tongues of

flame licked around the new log, and in seconds the fire was drawn straight up into the body of the stove.

So *that* is how the tiles are warmed, Mary thought, that is how the stove radiates heat. She stepped closer to examine the dramatic paintings on each tile, the sculptured figures separating them.

Rising, Angelica said, "My father created these tiles from the poems of Vergil, the great Roman poet. You see?" She pointed to a scene that might have been from the first book of the Old Testament itself. "The creation of the world."

In the lower border the poet's verse flowed in Latin script that only an artist could have achieved. Mary *wished* she could read it.

"The last tile will be an assembling of the ages since the Creation. And of prayers for peace for all mankind." Beckoning to Mary, Angelica glided around the gleaming tile cylinder.

The sculptured figures separating each panel were of kings and princes, shepherds and slaves, merchants and craftsmen. The folds of their garments were so real that Mary reached out to touch a figure.

Angelica's warning was too late. Mary drew back quickly from the scorching heat and stared at the inflamed surface of her palm. The stove was very hot!

Angelica rushed from the room, returning swiftly with an apothecary jar. "If you injure yourself when you are here," she cried, "you will surely not be permitted to return!" She spread an herb-scented lotion on Mary's palm and laid over it a square of soft flannel.

"Your glove will hold it in place," she advised as Mary drew the woolen mitten over her fingers.

From what seemed far away a church bell chimed through the sudden stillness.

Angelica sighed. "It is late, and I fear you must leave me now." She slipped Mary's coat from the chair. "But there is still so much that I must show you. Especially the kilns."

Her face was in shadow as she pleaded, "You have not promised to keep our secret, Maria."

Mary thought, If I could come back here, I would promise almost anything. She said, "I promise." But she could not shake the specter of the yellow monster hovering over the houses. "How long must I keep our secret?"

"Until my father comes."

"When will that be? Did the coachman tell you?"

They were moving toward the door; Mary felt

the cold draft from the cellar as Angelica lifted the latch.

"Very soon. Perhaps a day or two."

"How wonderful!" Mary said. "Perhaps my father will be here soon, too."

There was no answer to those last words. The door was closing between them, the flame casting tangled shadows around Angelica as she drifted away. Her voice faded. "Come back tomorrow! Please, my friend."

Mary glanced over her shoulder when she reached the corkscrew staircase. The shadowed cavern of the doorway had dwindled to a pencil-slim slit in the wall; the wavering light had disappeared.

7

The Sixteenth-Century Cap

Mary slipped out past the front door just as the yellow truck clanked over the cobblestones toward its nighttime hiding place, wherever that was. The snow must have driven them off, she thought. She *hoped*.

Looking back at the row of shuttered houses, she was shocked to see that the corner house was lower and more jagged than before. It was roped off now and surrounded with rubble.

She groaned aloud, wishing she had not promised Angelica she would keep their secret.

And, oh dear! It must be later than she had realized. The sky was the color of dark gray charcoal paper. What time *was* it?

Her watch was of no help because she had forgotten to adjust it to the corresponding Swiss hour yesterday. Its hands pointed to ten o'clock, which was ridiculous.

Halfway across the cobbled square on the way to the arch she remembered the cathedral clock. At the precise moment she craned her neck upward, a bell pealed. Through the snow she could barely see the clock's hands on the high tower. But she heard the bells.

Four!

She streaked over the slippery pavements, already filmed in frost. But now it was not so easy to get through the town. Shoppers, workers, cars, bikes, and buses crammed the narrow lanes, even the long hill road.

At Aunt Rosa's gateway she was not prepared for the bike that catapulted out of the snow mist, coming full speed through the open gate.

The boy braked so fast that his tires squealed and skidded.

He cried *"Achtung!"* a little late, swerving to avoid a collision.

Me watch out? Mary thought as she circled around him. What about you? She sent him a scathing look, but it did not daunt the boy, and Mary could not repress a giggle. His hair looked

44

as though he had forgotten to comb it; his nose was redder than his shining cheeks.

He grinned back at her, raised a hand, called out, *"Salu!"* and pedaled on into the hill road.

Aunt Rosa, already home from the museum, stood watching from the doorway. "That was Paul Huber, the neighbor's boy." She drew Mary inside. "Hurry on in. It's getting chillier every minute. You must have something warm to drink."

Mary almost said, "I've had something." But she was speechless. She was staring down at the hand from which she had removed her mitten.

How odd, she thought. What had happened to the delicate lotion and the square of flannel Angelica had placed so carefully on her scorched palm?

There was nothing wrong with that hand now, no feeling of any burn, no hint of the fragrance, no flannel in sight. Puzzled, she shook her mitten upside down, peered into it.

She slipped her hand back into her pocket and took out the iron key. Then she thought of the Angelica doll, but she waited until her aunt moved off toward the kitchen before she dug down into her pocket again.

45

What had happened? The pocket into which she had carefully tucked the doll was empty!

She laid the key on the edge of the umbrella stand, beneath the coat hangers. Then she pulled her pockets inside out. There was nothing at all in either pocket, not even the fold of silk.

For a moment she was too upset to think. Finally she leaned over and lifted the hem of her jumper.

Nothing had been cut from it. The hem was just as deep and straight as when her mother had turned it up.

"Looking for something, dear?" Aunt Rosa paused in the doorway.

"Yes—er—no." Until that instant Mary had not thought about all the complications of keeping the secret room a *secret*. She had been too occupied with getting back to Aunt Rosa's.

Now she was a little confused.

Reaching up to hang her coat on the wall hook, she bumped her knee against the umbrella stand. She winced, only then recalling how she had stumbled on the stone step. *She really had been inside Grandma's house alone!*

And certainly the room was there, at the bottom of the corkscrew staircase, just as Grandma had said.

Wasn't it?

She had met a girl named Angelica Biondi. Hadn't she?

Now she wished she had brought home a seed-cake or a piece of black bread.

But if the doll and the flannel had disappeared. . .

"Dreaming, Mary?" Aunt Rosa's words seemed to come from far away.

Mary shook her head. "I was just thinking about"—she hesitated—"the old houses, and the old streets." How difficult it was to choose the right words!

"Picturesque, aren't they?"

"Umm-hmm." Mary nodded. "Sort of like a fairy tale."

"I know." Aunt Rosa sounded a little sad. "*Outside,* that is. But those charming houses are so cold and damp inside." She shivered. "And so dark."

Mary did not say what she was thinking: *But in one of them there's a warm tile stove and honeycomb candles* . . .

Or was there?

She stood at the window gazing out at the darkening town, thinking that she really ought to forget the wonderful afternoon, at least for tonight. If she walked around in a dream, Aunt Rosa would suspect something, and, after all, Mary must keep the secret. She had promised Angelica.

In the meantime, Aunt Rosa must have been talking, and Mary had not been listening.

"You haven't heard a word I've said," Aunt Rosa declared. She moved closer, placed the back of her hand against Mary's cheek. "Maybe you're overtired," she said gently. "It might be wise for you to stay in bed tomorrow."

"Oh, no! I can't! I've got to go—" Mary bit her lip, then mumbled, "I've got to go down to town. There's so much to see."

"We'll talk about that in the morning." Aunt Rosa started to peel apples while Mary remained at the window.

If only her aunt knew, she thought. If only I could tell her.

"I meant to tell you this morning," her aunt said. "Your grandmother found your cap in a secret place in the old house."

"A—a secret place?" Mary turned, her words barely a whisper.

Aunt Rosa nodded. "She never told us where. Your mother and I longed to look for that place."

Mary stared up at her aunt. "Didn't you ever *ask* to go inside the house?"

Aunt Rosa nodded. "Yes, yes, of course we did. But the disagreeable old man who lived there refused to speak to us."

Mary burst out then. "Why did Grandma's parents sell the house?"

"Your mother and I wondered that, too, when we were your age," Aunt Rosa replied. "We always wished they hadn't."

"But *why*?" Mary persisted.

"You see, dear," Aunt Rosa explained, "Grandma's father died when she was no older than you. And her mother just couldn't afford to keep the house."

Mary thought she saw a tear slip down her aunt's cheek as she added, "Grandma's mother's only skill helped her through those bad days. She moved to a small flat and became a dressmaker. She put Grandma through school that way. And Grandma worked, too."

"What did she do?"

"Fine needlework. As fine as the work on your cap. She helped her mother." Aunt Rosa dried her hands and moved over to Mary. She traced the design on the embroidered cap. Her voice was low, hesitant. "I thought that your grandmother might have made this cap herself. It was only when I grew up that I learned the truth.

That cap belongs in a museum. It was handwoven and embroidered three hundred years ago.''

Her aunt smiled then. Her next words sent a peculiar chill up Mary's spine. ''The little girl who wore it hundreds of years ago must have been very much like you.''

8

The Door Is Locked!

Mary fell asleep that night praying for a blizzard so that none of the wrecking crew could get near the old houses, at least until Angelica's father came home. *Then* maybe she could tell Aunt Rosa and Mother and Father—if they had come to Wintertal by that time—all about the secret room.

Her prayer was answered! Next morning she awakened to the hum of snowplows chugging up the long hill road.

She bounced out of bed and was fully dressed and braiding her hair when Aunt Rosa came in especially early to ask whether she would like some hot *muesli* for breakfast. Mary was super-delighted to hear that Aunt Rosa had a meeting with the museum directors that morning.

That meant Mary would be able to go off on her own again!

But after breakfast and household chores were over, Aunt Rosa called out, "Wait a second, Mary!" Her aunt came out of her bedroom, carrying a wallet and a grocery list. "We need a few things for lunch," she said. "Director Forrer is coming, and because of our meeting this morning I won't have time to do any marketing."

Mary stamped on her boots a little harder than was absolutely necessary. Well, she supposed that having any extra time to herself was too good to be true.

"Both shops are near the market square." Aunt Rosa gave Mary the names and a list. "And since you'll probably reach home before we do, here's an extra key." She took one from a drawer in her secretary. "Or would you rather come to the museum and join us?"

Dropping Aunt Rosa's key into her pocket, Mary said "No, thank you" so quickly that her aunt laughed.

"Just like your grandmother," Aunt Rosa said. "You do remind me so much of her."

Aunt Rosa extracted a ten franc note from her

wallet and folded up two string bags for Mary. "Mind you," she said, "the packages won't be heavy, but they'll be bulky. I wonder whether Paul Huber can help."

Mary said nothing.

Mary heard the front door open and close. With an effort she restrained herself from dashing after her aunt. Anyway, what excuse could she give? She couldn't very well say, "I don't want help. I don't want to meet that Paul Huber. At least, not yet." Could she?

And now it was too late. Aunt Rosa must have found Paul right outside. Metal clattered against the stone house, and voices blew into the hall with a powder of snow and fresh, cold air.

Beyond her aunt and the boy as they stood in the open doorway Mary noticed the runner of a sled propped against the outer wall. Something stirred inside her. If she had not made other plans, that sled might have tempted her.

"Mary," her aunt said, "this is the boy I've been wanting you to meet, Paul Huber." Paul's face broke into a wide grin.

"*Ja,* Fräulein Biondi, I have seen your niece before." With a hearty *"Willkommen!"* he whipped off a mitten and shook her hand so vigorously that Mary almost shouted "Ow!"

Then Paul ran his fingers through his rebellious

53

hair. He looked so comical that Mary could hardly suppress a laugh, and Paul grinned again. "You speak English, please?" he said then. "I like to practice."

Mary blinked. "Yes, but maybe sometimes I could say something in your Swiss German."

Paul nodded, and shifted from one booted foot to another as snow melted onto the tile floor. Muttering a few words about almost running into her yesterday, he finally drew a deep breath and blurted out, "My mother thought maybe you'd like to go sledding."

Mary would have said, "Not now, thank you," but Aunt Rosa answered for her.

"You could be very helpful to us this morning, Paul. And my niece would enjoy a ride on your sled, too. I've just asked her to do a little marketing for us."

Paul watched Aunt Rosa warily as she went on. "You could ride the sled down to town on the Bergli path. And I'd be grateful if you'd help Mary carry back the packages."

Although Paul mumbled the Swiss equivalent of "Yes, ma'am," his expression left little doubt that he was not exactly pleased with the proposal.

By that time Mary felt sorry for him. But she did not say a word until they had crossed the hill road, Paul dragging the sled behind him on its rope.

"You don't *have* to come," she muttered then. "I can find my own way." But she was staring down the hill at the white crisp snow, barely touched by sled runners or footprints. Suddenly she hoped he wouldn't desert her. There had not been much snow in Boston during the past winter.

"Oh, it's all right," he said without looking at her. "I can go up to the big hill later."

She noticed that he had said "I," not "We," and she was relieved and disappointed at the same time.

They shoved off onto the curving path. With the feel of the cold wind on her cheeks, the lift of it in her hair, Mary forgot everything but admiration for Paul!

He steered like an expert, leaning at the curves like a proper tobogganer. And he braked—with the heels of his boots—to an exciting stop at the bottom, well clear of the busy thoroughfare.

At the sidewalk he leapt to his feet. "Okay," he said, which surprised her a little. She didn't think anyone in Switzerland would say okay. "Bakery's the first stop."

"You don't have to help me, really," Mary

insisted. "I—I won't mind." She had almost said, "I won't tell."

"Listen," he said, "as long as I've come this far, I might as well go on." He beckoned her to follow him as the traffic light turned green. "Anyway, now that I'm down here I'll go over and watch the work on the old buildings."

"The work?" Mary said.

"Ja," Paul went on. "They're knocking down some old buildings with a special machine from Zurich."

Mary kicked a chunk of ice across the pavement. "They won't be working today. There's too much snow," she said.

He stared at her. "I wouldn't be too sure. There's plenty of snow-clearing equipment here in Wintertal. It may be shoveled away already."

Mary's heart did a little flip. The snow had stopped, but she had been depending upon the drifts to prevent the swift return of that monstrous yellow crane.

"I want to go, too," she said. "Let's hurry."

Together, they raced to the bakery in Tor Street. The sled behind them bounced over the curbs, glided over the icy areas, and screeched over the clear spots on the pavements.

"Whew!" Paul panted when they reached the bakery shop. "What's your rush?"

"Well"—Mary blocked the door—"I want to see that machine from Zurich, too."

"Oh, it'll be there for a while."

"How long, do you think?" She was almost afraid to hear his answer.

"A week, maybe."

"A *week?*" Her voice squeaked in the quiet shop as the door opened. And it was worse once they were inside. The bakery smelled like Grandma's old house, like the secret room. Like hot crusty bread and spicy cakes. Mary felt an ache creep around her heart.

She murmured, *"Sechs Brötchen, bitte,"* to the woman behind the counter. She turned to Paul. "Only a week?" she prodded.

He shrugged. "I don't know. My father says those cranes are very powerful."

Mary pushed the warm rolls into the market bag and scooped up the silver coins from the counter. "Come *on,*" she urged.

If she had felt she had more time that morning, she might have lingered in the little supermarket across the street. It was different from the ones in Boston, smaller, and instead of pushcarts there were only red baskets to carry. But the shelves offered nearly as many tempting items. And, thank goodness, Paul knew where everything was.

In no time they were at one of the two checkout counters paying for the rice and aluminum foil and milk and flavoring salt.

Outside, Paul tied the two packages onto the sled. Then he raced along after Mary, who had already started toward Neumarkt and the archway.

"I didn't know girls liked such things, all that smashing and noise and dirt," he called after her.

"I don't!" she flung back. "I'd stop it if I could. I think it's awful, just *awful!*"

"Don't be silly," he said. "Didn't your aunt tell you about Wintertal's 'centuries of progress' plan?"

They had to slow down on the cobbles of the marketplace. It was slippery and bumpy before they entered the archway. Paul drew up beside her then. "They're nothing but a lot of old houses, anyway. Nobody needs them anymore."

"What do you mean?" Mary's voice vibrated in the low, dark tunnel. " 'Centuries of progress'! It's stupid if you don't preserve some things to show what you're supposed to have progressed from. Besides, *my* father says most old buildings are much better constructed than new ones."

Paul sent her a quick glance. "You're funny," he said. Then, after a moment, he added, "But really, we need more room here for people and schools and things like that.''

''There's plenty of room out *there*.'' She swept her arm back toward the hill. They had swerved and curved past a lot of emptiness on the sled coming down that hill. ''I don't understand,'' she added.

They came out from beneath the archway into the cathedral square. The snow crunched under their boots as they started across.

Today there was not even a pigeon where the gardens had been. There was not even a garden. There were white mounds and white-frosted gates and white-laced steeples and eaves. Snow was piled up so high in the half-demolished house that it looked like a gigantic box of powdered sugar with the top torn off.

Mary was indignant because no passerby paused to look at the row of history that was doomed to vanish from their lives.

Paul didn't look, either. He and his sled were ahead of her and halfway across the square when she saw the gigantic scoop swing around the corner at the end of Church Lane. Metal clanged as it struck the cobbles. It chugged, huffed, and deposited a pile of snow from the street on top of the mound in the truck.

''See?'' Paul looked back at her. He pointed

to the snowplow. "The Zurich crane will soon be at work!"

"Why don't you go over and see what they've done already," Mary called out bitterly. His cheerful attitude annoyed her more than ever.

She had already noticed that there was no smoke from the chimney of the pink house, and it worried her.

When Paul disappeared around the cathedral, she glanced up and down the street, then darted into the recessed doorway of Grandma's house. Her mittened hand fastened on the iron knob, and she shoved hard.

The door did not move.

Recalling her first experience with this door, she grasped the iron knocker. But this time when it dropped, the door did not swing open even an inch. In fact, it sounded lonely and hollow.

Mary was not exactly frightened, but she was apprehensive. She peered over her shoulder to be sure that Paul had not spied her retreat. Now was her chance to try her key for the first time!

She dug into her pocket for it, the pocket where she had kept it for the past few days.

It was not there!

With pounding heart she fumbled to see whether it might have worn a hole. But, no. The pocket was as good as new.

In the other pocket she found Aunt Rosa's small modern brass key, that was all.

Oh! How terrible it would be if she had lost that key! What would she do? Would she *ever* get back into the room again?

She gripped the doorknob, tried to shake it. But nothing shook or rattled. The door did not budge. As Father had said, so many old buildings were built to last forever.

She leaned back, then, hoping for a glimpse of reassuring smoke from the second chimney. She leaned so far back that she fell off the step and sat down—*plop!*—in a snowbank.

A voice exploded behind her. "Well, here she is again!" It was the man she had met yesterday, the supervisor. "It's the same young one," he muttered.

Strong arms lifted her to her feet. Mumbling her thanks, Mary avoided the man's arms while she brushed off the snow. She held her breath, too, waiting for his scolding.

"Little one," he chided, "you'll have to keep away from these houses, or you might get hurt."

Me get hurt? Mary almost cried out. *You* don't know! She wanted to shout, You're going to crush a beautiful room—and *people*—to smithereens! Oh! Keeping Angelica's secret was unbearable.

61

When she peered up at the man, his face was misty through the tears that stung her eyes.

"Ho, ho!" He misinterpreted the tears. "Your fall must have been harder than I thought." Then, obviously to cheer her up, he added, "Not wandering around in the cellar anymore, are you?" The deep voice ended in a chuckle.

Mary scowled, resenting his merriment.

Out of the corner of her eyes she noticed movement behind the man. Paul's bright blue eyes stared at her in something like amazement.

"What did you do?" the man prodded good-naturedly. "Leave your key at home on the television set? Eh?"

That was it! She *had* left the iron key on the umbrella stand in Aunt Rosa's hall last evening.

Without waiting for Paul or the bags full of groceries, she started to run back toward Aunt Rosa's house.

9

Disappeared?

Mary had almost reached the hill road before she heard the sled bump and scrape behind her.

"Allo!" Paul cried when he caught up with her at a traffic light. "What was *that* all about?"

"Nothing," Mary muttered, as annoyed with herself as she was with him and the supervisor.

"What do you mean, 'nothing'? Were you really down in the cellar of that house?"

"Well—er—" she stammered. "Well, yes." She wished he would stop asking questions.

"How did you get in?"

"The door didn't seem to be locked." In a sense that was true, but she was not pleased with her evasive excuse.

As they crossed the busy intersection together, she noticed the number of people and cars and trucks buzzing about. If trucks could move, the crane and its crew might be crashing around down in the square. Her spirits fell even lower when she realized that the snow was melting around the edges.

Paul glanced sideways at her as he yanked the sled along. "I suppose they locked that old front door after they caught you."

"It certainly was locked up tight." She hoped she sounded discouraged so he would stop the steady flow of questions. But he persisted.

"What was down in the cellar?" he whispered.

"Not much." She dared not mention the firewood, nor of course, anything else.

"Could you *see?*"

"A little." She paused. Then, still hoping to discourage him, she added, "Hardly at all."

"I've got a flashlight," he said promptly. "Why don't we investigate?"

Something happened inside Mary. She felt violently protective about her secret. She did not want this boy or the supervisor or *anyone* to step into her private realm. Not yet.

Stiffly she said, "I told you the door's locked. I just tried it."

Paul hesitated only slightly before he went on. "There are other houses in the block." He waited, and when she did not comment, he added, "Maybe someone left something behind. Buried treasure . . . a chest full of gold?"

"Oh, don't be silly," Mary snapped. She wished he would stop.

Paul was persistent. "There could be a secret panel."

Warnings zigzagged through Mary's mind. She would have to put him off somehow, or he might get in her way. His very presence might prevent her return to Angelica and their room. She remembered with a shiver how the supervisor's entrance into Grandma's house had banished the light and the warmth.

With an effort she attempted a flippant answer. "What an imagination you have!"

"I know." They were hustling through the gateway to the garden apartments when Paul, unabashed, went on, "I may go back there later today."

Mary swung around so fast that she almost knocked him down. "I thought you were going sledding up on the big hill."

"Oh, I can do both." At Aunt Rosa's door he untied the groceries and thrust them at her. *"Auf*

Wiedersehen!" He raised his mittened hand in a goodbye gesture before he swished off over the snow-covered garden.

For the moment, as Mary watched Paul retreat toward his own door, she forgot the key. She forgot everything but her own fear.

In a daze she rang Aunt Rosa's bell before she recalled that her aunt's brass key was actually in her pocket. She was fumbling for it when she heard a loud *clank* inside the hall.

Mary burst into the hall just as her aunt picked up the old iron key from the tile floor near the umbrella stand.

"It's mine!" she cried. She thrust the groceries onto the table and ran across the hall.

Aunt Rosa stared from the elaborate key to Mary, watching her fingers close on the smooth shaft.

"That's an old key," Aunt Rosa said. "I suppose Grandma gave it to you."

Mary nodded, slipping it quickly into her pocket, where it belonged.

"Looks like one of the keys to the old Biondi house," her aunt went on. "I remember one or two like that, but little good they did us. We'd never dare try one."

"Why not?"

"The house didn't belong to the family anymore, remember."

Mary looked at Aunt Rosa thoughtfully. "Who owns it right now?" she asked.

"The Town Council." Suddenly Aunt Rosa swooped up the packages Mary had dropped on the hall table. "Lunch!" she said. "For goodness' sake, Director Forrer is coming. I've got to braise the veal. And thank you, dear, for bringing the rice."

Who was Director Forrer? Mary wondered. She trailed after her aunt and asked her.

"The secretary of the Town Council, and quite important in the museum, as well. He's coming to report on the results of our meeting. By the way, he'll be very interested in your cap and that old key. The museum is looking for just such fine old artifacts."

Mary was not very happy about having lunch with a man who was involved in the destruction in the old town and who might want to collect her cap and key.

She was silent. Her feelings about her aunt wavered again, and she decided she would not like Director Forrer any more than she liked that old supervisor.

But when the director came a half hour later,

Mary was astonished to find that he was just a man like her father or the principal of her school in Boston, or—well, just a man.

As a matter of fact, he was more polite than the principal and most other men. He sort of bowed when he shook hands, and his grip was as hard as Paul's. Nevertheless, she was glad she had carefully folded her cap in tissue paper and hidden it in the back of her drawer.

And she hoped that her aunt would not mention the cap or the key. If this man wanted either or both of them, she just didn't know what she would do.

It was her aunt's mention of a tile stove that caught her attention. She sat up straighter, waiting for Director Forrer's answer.

"I'm afraid you'll find the 1695 stove in Tal Castle is the oldest one in good condition in this area, Fräulein Biondi."

"That seems very odd," Aunt Rosa said. "When I was a child, we learned in school that tile artists settled here one hundred years before that. Our mother told us that an ancestor of ours came here from the Engadine Valley before 1600."

"I know." He nodded. "The famous Anton Biondi."

Mary closed her eyes. He is speaking of Angelica's father, she thought. She could see the secret room, the beautiful stove, Angelica . . . She thought: How can I keep her secret? How?

Then she heard Director Forrer say, "I am ashamed to admit that Wintertal has been foolish enough to sell whatever we could find of Biondi's fine work. For good prices, mind you, but that's no excuse."

No, it isn't, Mary almost muttered. But when he added, "We often learn too late that money can't replace what history had left us," she stared openly at him.

Director Forrer was looking at Aunt Rosa now. "And worse than selling for profit," he said, "two priceless Biondi treasures have simply disappeared."

"Disappeared?" Her aunt frowned.

The director nodded. "His finest creations. One, a magnificent stove, each panel a painting of an episode of one of Vergil's poems, and—"

Mary held her breath.

"—and something so unique that it was mentioned in our town's oldest records. A perfect duplicate of the Biondi house. A doll's house."

Mary dropped her fork then—*ping!*—onto her plate. She was so embarrassed, so upset, but she controlled herself. She did not blurt out: *But it's*

69

there! They're both down there in the secret room!

Oh! How she wished she dare say it, wished she had not promised Angelica, wished she were *sure!*

She had to get back to Grandma's house in a hurry. She had to!

10

The Key

It seemed hours to Mary before she finally managed to leave the table without appearing rude. In her own room she crammed her cap into one pocket, key into the other, and raced along to the front hall.

While she was putting on her boots, the few words she overheard only added to her agitation.

Director Forrer and her aunt had evidently been discussing the cap and key, for Aunt Rosa said, "I'm sure Mary wouldn't mind showing them to you, although she *is* very attached to them."

Mary did not wait to hear another word. She

plunged out the front door and rushed down the path into the long hill road as though the director were after her.

Once out of sight of the house, she whipped the cap from her pocket and tied it over her braids.

She put on an extra spurt of speed when she saw the enormous snowplow lurch past the cathedral. The street was almost clear of snow! That yellow crane with its swinging iron ball could be back at any moment!

Before Mary had time to insert the iron key in the lock, the door to Grandma's house swung open. She closed it behind her, raced across the hall, and hurried down the corkscrew staircase. Beyond the partly open door at the far end of the cellar, she glimpsed Angelica leaning over the threshold of the secret room, holding the candle high.

Mary drew a deep and shaky breath. Then she stared at her friend. How different she looked!

Her dark hair fell softly around her face, curving over her lace collar.

The girls stood motionless, Angelica staring at Mary's braids, and Mary staring at Angelica's modern hairdo. The door swung shut on the echoes of their laughter, but once inside the secret room, Mary grew serious again.

"Angelica, there's so little time!" She thrust an arm back, pointing toward the cellar outside. "They—the Town Council—are going to destroy everything! They don't know about the room! They think your tile stove and doll's house have disappeared!"

She leaned past Angelica just to be sure the tile stove was still there.

It was. *And it was complete!* Below the lovely pastoral scene, the artist's signature was intertwined with laurel and alpine roses:

Anton Biondi
1583

Mary's mouth dropped open. She stared around at Angelica. *1583!*

There was something else different about Angelica today, a twinkle in her eyes, a glow about her. Something wonderful must have happened.

She heard a soft *thud* from outside the room.

No! She thought. It can't be Paul! He couldn't have followed me! She glanced quickly over her shoulder, but Angelica whispered, "Do not be alarmed, Mary. Come."

"But didn't you hear that?" Mary answered. "I might have been *followed!*"

Angelica was laughing now. She glided soundlessly toward the next room, the room Mary had not seen. Before she touched the latch, however, the door flew open.

The man who stepped into the light was as tall as Mary's father, but so very different, with his thick dark hair and sweeping mustache. Different, too, were his long fitted jacket of the same coarse woven fabric as Angelica's frock and his knee breeches, dark as the green of the forest.

Cradled in his hands was a miniature tile stove exactly the shape of the stove in the secret room.

Seeing Mary, he instantly set down the little stove on the table and curved his free arm around Angelica. At this affectionate gesture her smile actually seemed to brighten the room.

"So this is Mary," the man said almost to himself, although his eyes searched Mary's. "So you are the one."

Mary gazed up at him. "I beg your pardon, sir?" She had been thinking: So this is Angelica's father.

Anton Biondi laughed aloud, a sound so merry that Mary laughed as well. Then, to his daughter he murmured, "She is a very proper little one, isn't she?"

"She is my friend—our friend." Angelica looked up into his eyes as though to remind him of a secret they both shared.

There was a slow change in his expression. He glanced away, behind his daughter, as though he were contemplating something Angelica could not see, something far away.

And when his dark, penetrating eyes returned to Angelica and to her, Mary felt a slight stir of air above her shoulders as he passed a hand over her cap and braids.

"We are fortunate to have a friend like you. Especially now," he said. His gaze moved over the room, lingered on the tall, gleaming tile stove, on the doll's house. Abruptly he asked, "You have the key, of course?"

Mary drew it from her pocket, held it in her palm. Although she did not feel the touch of his fingers, she felt the key lift as Anton Biondi took it from her.

"Tell me." He searched her eyes. "Who gave you this?"

"My grandmother." Then, shyly, Mary added, "She lived here, in this house." She untied the streamers of her cap and removed it from her head. "Grandmother found this, here in this room, long ago." She held out the cap to Angelica. "It belongs to you, not to *them*."

Anton Biondi pulled his daughter a little closer; his eyes held Mary's. "Of whom do you speak?"

"The—the Town Council," Mary stammered.
"They—they need things for the museum." She
looked around desperately. "They want that,
too." She pointed at the handsome stove. "And
that." She nodded at the doll's house beside it.

Her eyes pleaded with him. How could she
ask him to understand when she did not?

"They've been searching for all the old things.
They want everything they've lost. But—but—
they're going to—" She simply could not utter
the words "destroy the house, itself."

Anton Biondi seemed to understand without
further words from her. A sadness touched his
brilliant eyes, faint lines appeared between his
black brows. The arm that held Angelica close
to his side trembled slightly.

Angelica broke the silence. *"You* must keep
the cap, Mary. It belongs to you now." She
glanced at her father as though for approval.

"Yes," Anton Biondi said to Mary. "It is
yours. That, and more. Part of your heritage, a
small part, but I need not remind you. You will
protect them." He seemed only then to be aware
of the exquisite replica of the tile stove he had
placed on the table.

He lifted it, and he and Angelica silently
moved to the open doll's house and knelt upon
the floor.

Mary stared.

There was an addition to the doll's house! There was a basement below it now, a copy of the long cellar of Grandma's house! There was a miniature corkscrew staircase!

And, at the rear, extending *beyond* the house—of all things—was *the secret room!* Oddly, there was no cover to the room, no ceiling. She could see straight down into it, like a bird's-eye view.

Everything was in its correct place: chests, table, chairs, recessed doors. Everything except the copy of the beautiful tile stove.

While she watched, Anton Biondi set the tiny stove into the empty corner.

"You see," Anton Biondi said softly to his daughter, "our young friend has come just in time."

Mary felt a drift of air as Angelica's fingers brushed hers. "This is what I have been waiting for, Mary," she whispered. "Here is my father's workroom."

Larger than the secret room, the wall adjoining the miniature cellar was filled by a strange conical fireplace that looked like half of a funnel turned upside down.

"My father's kiln." Angelica touched the little copy of a brick-baking fireplace.

The fireplace, or kiln, as Angelica had called

it, leaned against the wall of the kiln room just below the rear wall of the pink house. Surrounded to the ceiling by racks and shelves, its chimney broke through the rear wall of the doll's house and joined the main flue.

Twin chimneys extended up through all three stories and emerged at the rippled roof.

There *was* a second chimney! She *had* seen it, had seen the smoke rising from it.

When she could find the words, Mary turned from the doll's house to the smaller door in the secret room. "Is the *real* kiln in there, past that door?" She looked from Angelica to her father.

Anton Biondi rose, drew his daughter to her feet, and with one arm around her started toward the kiln room.

But Angelica pulled back and, turning, held out her hand to Mary. Her eyes seemed enormous in her delicate round face and, like her father's, no longer merry.

"Must we leave Mary so soon?" Her appeal to Anton Biondi was answered by silence except for the lift of the latch beneath his fingers, the sigh of hinges as the door opened away from them. Mary saw, too, that he held his daughter closely, guiding her over the threshold into the room beyond.

At first their figures blocked the view, and although Mary moved quickly to the doorway, she saw them merge with their surroundings: kiln, clay, tiles, loom.

A whole new world unfolded before her.

She clung to the door, staring.

It was exactly like the doll's house duplicate of the kiln room. But now she could see and hear and smell the log fire crackling in the kiln's open hearth. She could almost touch the unglazed tiles drying on the surrounding shelves.

The smell of clay blended with the colors, oils, and resins. Their pungence mingled with the aromas of black bread cooling on its rack, beeswax hardening in the crude candle molds.

Close by on a wooden loom, a length of plain cloth stretched from roller to beam. Angelica's loom, Angelica's yarn basket beside it.

On top lay a cap of the same wool as Mary's, partially embroidered. The heavy needle slanted through an unfinished leaf, glinting in the firelight.

Sudden tears stung Mary's eyes. Angelica gave me her cap, she thought, because she was making another!

"Mary," Angelica murmured softly from beside her father, "all this belongs to you, remember."

She held out her hands toward Mary once

more, but once more her father drew her back, away from Mary, away from the light.

The kiln towered above them, casting them into a strange blue shadow.

Mary blinked, closed her eyes, opened them cautiously. Angelica seemed so far away, blurred, her father a mere form beyond her.

"Don't go!" Mary stepped into the room, but it was as though a wind had picked up her voice and driven it back. A cold wind, damp as a sea-fog and as misty.

Wait! Mary wanted to cry. Don't go! We must stop those people outside. We must stop that crane! That iron ball must not strike again!

But she could not utter a sound. Like the wind that had silenced her voice, a silver veil now descended between them, and she was alone in a vast forgotten cave where echoes themselves would defeat her.

Even as she peered through the encroaching darkness, she saw the walls crust with twilight. Or was it dust motes drifting, settling?

The room around her grew colder, darker; the colors vanished, the fire flattened on the hearth, turning to ashes as she watched.

Into the peculiar silence that held her motionless, she heard a distant *bong-g-g,* then another and another. At the fourth count, Mary cried, "It's late! I must go!"

But there was no answer, no soft voice calling out to her, no restraining hand holding her back.

There was no one in the kiln room!

She backed slowly through the doorway to the secret room, paused there, peered into the gloom.

She tried to cry out, "Come back! Come back! Angelica!" Her lips formed the words, but no sound came, and no answer.

The kiln room before her and the secret room behind her were dark and very cold.

Blindly Mary turned, stumbled across the stone floor, and pulled open the heavy door that led back to the cellar.

11

The Sign of the Sculptor

The instant the door closed behind her, Mary remembered the key. She swung around and flung herself back against what should have been the carved door.

But there was no door. There was only rough stone, musty and snow-cold.

"Angelica!" She cried. *"Angelica!"* She beat her fists, scraped her fingernails against the gritty surface, scrabbled on the little peaks and scratches in the stone.

"Your father's got the key!" she shouted. "I need the key!" When only silence answered her, she spread her arms, traced every inch of the wall that she could reach. Finally with bruised fingers and aching arms, she leaned against the wall and closed her eyes.

"Mary . . . all this belongs to you, remember. . . ." The voice was so soft, so far away, that it could have been a mere memory, an echo of Angelica's. But Mary's pulse quickened.

"Mary-y-y—"

She's there! Mary thought. She'll come! Excited, she pressed her ear against the wall.

"Mary-y-y-y—"

Mary whirled around, stared back toward the staircase. That cry came from above, from outside. It came again.

"Mary! Are you in there?" Now the cry was interspersed with pounding.

She felt cornered. Paul had found her! She'd known he would. Oh, he must not make a scene out there! He must not bring the workmen to the house!

She flew across the black cellar, struck the first step with the toe of her boot, and pitched forward. The cutting edge of the stone against her shin sobered her.

Patience, she reminded herself. If I wait long enough, and keep very quiet, he might go away. She tiptoed slowly up the remainder of the steps.

By the time she reached the top, the hammering had ceased; the voice was fainter, farther away. "Mary-y-y-y! Your aunt wants you!"

Oh! She was pulled in two directions! *What was she going to do about the key?*

The street outside was quiet when she slipped out past the front door into the gray afternoon. She had just reached the sidewalk when she heard Paul's cry from the corner.

"Allo! Allo!" Mary knew by now that this was a sort of combination of "Hello!" and "Hi!" and "Hey!" She tried to amble casually along while he sped toward her and slid to a stop.

"Your aunt sent me for you!" he said.

"Is it late?" She hoped she sounded normal, natural, but Paul gave her a penetrating look.

"It's late, all right, and it's going to rain. A real storm, the radio says. Your aunt wants you home."

Mary barely heard his last sentence. To the turmoil inside her, another fear was added. Rain would wash away all the snow and ice, and the crane would really start moving. Oh, dear, oh, dear! she thought, I've got to think of something!

Paul snapped his fingers before her eyes. "Say," he said, "did you hear me?"

She jerked her head away and gazed beyond him.

"You dream all the time," he muttered. "I never saw a girl like you." But there was a hint of mischief in his eyes when he added, "Guess where *I've* been!"

"Where?"

"Around the whole row of houses. There are old rundown stables in the back. Did you know that?"

Mary's mind did a snappy somersault. "Could we go and *see* them?" She thought, Maybe I'll find another entrance back there!

Paul glanced quickly at the sky. "Okay." He started off. "But let's hurry." He seemed pleased that he had discovered something she had overlooked.

She followed at his heels as he dashed past the row of houses and around the roped-off corner building. There, because the alley slanted down and was slippery and cluttered with rubble, they picked their way carefully until they reached a grimy door built flat into the stone wall.

"Here it is!" Paul grasped the rusty latch.

Mary doubted she would have investigated this area on her own. The door was very dirty and so narrow that she was sure that old supervisor could never have squeezed through.

Filthy or not, Paul put his shoulder against it and shoved.

The hinges gave way with such a miserable squawk that Mary glanced swiftly behind her to see whether anyone had heard them. But the lane was empty. And when she turned back, Paul was already swallowed up in the gloom beyond the door which had started to creak shut.

"Wait for me!" She pushed the door away from her, filled with misgivings now. The buildings, stables, whatever they were, seemed to lean together, and the lane was dreadfully dark and crammed with snow-crested litter.

She stepped over piles of splintered wood and broken stone and roof tiles and shattered glass left by the iron ball. "Wait!" she called out again.

"Well, hurry up, then!" Paul stopped and reached back his hand for her, and together they edged through the passage, past more low, ancient iron-bound doors. It smelled musty, a little like the basement outside the secret room a few moments ago.

She shuddered at the memory, embarrassed when Paul looked back, puzzled. "Are you cold?" he asked.

"No." She peered past him. "Look!"

"I know," he said matter-of-factly. "This is the stable courtyard."

She stumbled after him into the cobbled court, a wilderness of forgotten time, of low, single-storied buildings of half-timber and stone, darkened by age. Those few windows that opened onto the yard were small, crusted now with the grime of neglect like the walls she had seen in the kiln room after Angelica had left.

Over the wide metal-pegged doors of streaked and rotting wood hung lanterns more of dust than glass.

How old they looked, these lost, unwanted buildings, Mary thought, how useless. She stared in silence.

"They were stables, you know," Paul explained.

"When?"

"Hundreds of years ago. You can tell by the low doors."

"But, how—" Mary murmured, "—how did horses and carriages get in here?"

"That way." Paul nodded toward a wide archway straight ahead now sealed up with stone and timber crossbars. "Probably led to Friar's Lane. Hey! Look at *this* stuff!"

He pointed to a huddle of wrought-iron castings laced with snow. Leaning over, he disentangled one narrow piece and with his heavy glove brushed snow from the curving letters of a word.

It was part of the sign Mary had seen the first day when she had returned alone to the pink house. It was the word on the bracket over Grandma's front door.

"Bildhauer," Paul said. "If this belongs to that pink house, it means a sculptor lived there once."

Mary thought: Now I know what *Bildhauer* means. Anton Biondi had been a sculptor, a ceramic artist, maybe the finest in Wintertal.

She looked up at Paul, then around at the leaning ancient shed that jutted out from Grandma's house. "That was not the sculptor's house," she corrected softly, "that was his stable."

"Well, since horses have gone, they used them for storage sheds. Some people even lived in such places for a while." He shook his head, then added, "But not anymore. Before you know it—*whoom!*—they'll all be gone."

She turned her back on him and stepped over to the nearest window. With her folded-up handkerchief she scrubbed at the dirt-caked surface, trying to peer into the room or the shed beyond. But she could see nothing for the tears that blurred her eyes.

They can't! she thought. They just can't knock

down Grandma's house. Oh! I've got to get back in there!

"Say, come on!" Paul urged. "It's starting to rain."

Furtively Mary dabbed at her wet cheeks. Then she leaned down and tugged at the wrought-iron cutout of crusted letters BILDHAUER. With some difficulty she lifted the sign from the heap of cast-off decoration. It was bulky and heavy and dirty and wet. But she didn't care.

It belonged to Angelica and Anton Biondi. In a way, it belonged to Grandma and her mother and Aunt Rosa and her.

"We'd better get moving." Paul had already started back toward the entrance to the alley. When he reached the rubble-cluttered narrow path, he turned and thrust back his hand to clasp hers again.

Catching sight of the iron sign she had wrapped in her arms, he shouted, "You aren't taking *that* home?" His expression was so comical that Mary almost laughed. "What will your aunt say?"

"I think she'll like it." Mary struggled to shift it under one arm. "She's an artist, too. She does sketches and things for the museum sometimes."

"Here, let me help you," Paul said gruffly. He took one end of the cutout, and she held the other, and together they pitched and clanged their way through the side lane, across the old town and up the hill.

As they approached the gate to the row of garden apartments, they could see Aunt Rosa standing in the doorway of the building where she lived.

"See," Paul murmured under his breath. "She's looking for you. We'd better leave this old thing behind these bushes for tonight."

He pushed the sign of the sculptor down into the soft mixture of snow and slush just before they entered the gateway.

12

Alone

"Of all days for you to be late!" Aunt Rosa
said the moment Mary had thanked Paul and he
had trudged off to his own house. "And in this
rain! Suppose you catch cold now?"

She scowled down at Mary as she drew her
into the hallway. "Of all times, just when your
mother and father are ready to leave Egypt.
They're due here tomorrow."

Mary stared up at her aunt. She was not at all
certain that she wanted them to come here so
soon.

"And it was just too bad that you weren't here
when they telephoned," Aunt Rosa added. "I

had to explain to your mother that you were as fascinated by the old town as we had been.''

''What did she say?'' Mary asked.

''She laughed.''

Mary drew a deep breath. All was well with her world. At least her mother understood.

''She obviously trusts you.'' Aunt Rosa's arm went around Mary. ''I suppose you're hungry by now.''

Mary just remembered that she hadn't eaten any black bread or seedcakes today with Angelica. ''Yes, Aunt Rosa, I am.''

Maybe she ate too much of Aunt Rosa's delicious *Roesti,* those heavenly diced potatoes that were simmered in butter until they were crispy, and lamb cutlets and lovely chocolate dessert, but Mary didn't sleep very well that night. Or maybe it was the worries about Grandma's house.

All night long in the soft bed Mary shivered beneath the puffy feather quilt. That monstrous crane could be battering the house again even before Aunt Rosa called her for breakfast. She *had* to do something.

She simply had to go back to Grandma's house before the crane got there. She had to try once more to find Angelica before it was too late. She had to go, even if she didn't have the key. Now she was sorry she had given the key to Anton Biondi and had left it in the secret room.

She was out of bed long before anything stirred on the hill. In fact, beyond her window there were no lights in any of the houses as far as she could see.

The sky was as dark as Aunt Rosa's hall when she unlatched the front door and backed out onto the stone step. She kicked something that clanged slightly and peered down at the wrought-iron sign: BILDHAUER. It was braced against the stone flowerpot beside Aunt Rosa's door.

Paul must have carried it up from behind the bushes where he had hidden it last night. Mary glanced up at the house where he lived, hoping he had not heard her. Or did she? He wasn't so bad, after all. He had been a real help yesterday.

But his house was dark. No, a light flashed on, casting an oblong pattern on the snow-blotched lawn. And upstairs in the flat above Aunt Rosa's, a window clicked open or shut. Mary did not wait to find out.

She ran.

By the time she reached the marketplace, the light rain had stopped. Dawn was a pale thin streak of lemon yellow beyond the rooftops and surrounding hills. And farmers were setting up their stalls, shaking out their colorful umbrellas.

She weaved around them and sped through the archway.

At least the cathedral square was empty as it had been that first noontime when Grandma's house had appeared so strangely alive. Its sculptor's sign had been in place then, its trail of smoke had hovered over the steep roof.

She looked up now.

No sign hung from the iron bracket, of course.

No smoke, no wisp of silver curled into the cold, gold sky.

And her pocket was empty. She had no key.

13

The Hole in the Stone

All the way down the hill and through the town Mary had been taunted by a faint hope that she might find the door to Grandma's house unlatched.

But when she reached it, the door did not yield a fraction of an inch.

Standing on the stone step, cold and alone in the half-light of dawn, she could think of only one other possibility. The stable in the courtyard. Yesterday she had noticed doors that looked fragile, their hinges rusted enough to break off at a touch.

Something began to come to her; something about the location of the stable and the kiln room that had been eluding her all night. There had been no windows in the kiln room or in the secret room. In the doll's house model three rooms had been under and behind the house.

She darted around to the side lane, past the corner house, and was halfway down the slope when she heard the truck rumble over the cobbles in cathedral square.

A quick look over her shoulder was all she needed. That crane towered over the half-demolished corner house like a yellow dragon, ready to pounce.

Just as it rattled to a stop at the corner, Mary shoved at the grimy door Paul had found yesterday. It squawked inward, plunging her into the shadowed alley.

Although the rain had washed away the snow and ice, she still had to feel her way over the broken stone and glass. It was even more gloomy in the narrow passage than it had been yesterday, and lonely without Paul. The leaning old buildings closed her in. She paused, wondering whether she should turn back, whether she should give up.

No, she wouldn't. She looked ahead toward the wider courtyard at the end. There, in the semidarkness, loomed the blocked-off archway to Friar's Lane.

Blocked off?

Mary stopped right where she was.

Hadn't she read in many books about blocked-off doorways, secret entrances, hidden caves, smugglers' coves, sealed-off fireplaces? She shivered, not from the cold.

Could that have happened, somehow, for some strange reason *inside* the pink house? Could those two basement rooms have been blocked off and forgotten?

She stared up over the tumbled roof of the ancient stable that jutted out from Grandma's house. With its peeling paint, chipped uneven windows, broken shutters, and tilted chimney pots, it looked like a weird painting of a house where some mean old ogre might live. Prickles crept up Mary's spine.

The stable actually leaned against the house, pressed back by the weight of its sagging doors, by stacks of broken window frames and shutters.

Where was that oddly shaped chimney of the kiln room?

Inside the stable?

Impulsively she grasped the latch on the stable door. But her hand froze there.

Out in the side lane, at the end of the long alley behind her, she heard footsteps, voices, one distinct. "I thought I heard something move down this way."

It was the supervisor!

Mary recognized the hair-raising squeak of the alley door. She twisted the rusty loop of the iron latch on the stable door and wrenched. One weathered wooden door almost snapped off, it came away so easily.

The voices and steps ceased for a second. Then, *"Ja, ja,"* the supervisor said. "I was right. Come along."

Mary crept inside, pulled the door shut, held her breath while she waited. But, oh! the foul old ancient smells of dank earth and mildew! She hardly dared take her first step in the blackness that abruptly engulfed her.

Who knew what lay around her in this opaque gloom? Spiders, at least. A web clung to her fingers, another crossed her eyes. She shook them off and wiped her hand against her coat.

Gradually her eyes became accustomed to the darkness. She moved forward slowly, over flat broken stones, earth, rags. The toe of her boot tangled with cloth or canvas. She reached down, touched it.

Rotten burlap fell apart in her hands. Musty dust almost choked her. She pressed a finger tightly under her nose to prevent her sneeze.

The men were outside the stable now!

"There *was* a noise down here." The supervisor paused, then muttered, "There's been a young one hanging around this particular house. I wonder—"

The latch clicked behind Mary, and midway across the stable she swung around, bracing herself for the encounter.

Then, almost worse than being caught, was the other voice—*Director Forrer's voice*—and what he said! "Could be a rat. Or a bat."

A rat? Mary's skin crawled. She pulled her coat close, straining to listen over the thumping of her heart. She drew a shaky breath when the supervisor answered briskly, "No rats around here." He dropped the latch. "A stray cat, maybe." Footsteps grated on the stone outside as the men moved off.

Mary breathed more normally once more. She started to back away, peering in the direction of the door, though she could see nothing. She backed into the rear wall with a thud, stood rigidly waiting, wondering whether the men had heard.

But they had passed beyond her. Fragments of their conversation floated back; something about doors. Then silence, and she turned quickly and tapped the wall behind her.

This had to be the wall to Grandma's house, at least the wall of the stable that adjoined the house. She pressed her ear close as she thumped the palm of her hand hard along the damp stone.

Nothing. Nothing. Not a hollow spot as high as she could reach or as wide. At the end of the wall she struck a ladder, which she cautiously braced against the wall and climbed upon. She thumped the wall as high as the ceiling, then halted suddenly.

The voices were returning, the supervisor's quite clear. *"Nei, nei,* Herr Director," he said. "You wouldn't want any of these doors."

Mary shrank back as he tapped the stable door sharply.

"Bad condition, see?" he went on. "Warped and cracked."

The director's sigh was audible even to Mary. "Such neglect," he said. "A great pity."

"Well, sir," said the supervisor, "the last owner was an old skinflint. People say he only bought the place because there'd been rumor of hidden treasure."

"So I understand." Director Forrer's voice was solemn. "Probably angry when he found nothing and deliberately let the place run down."

Found nothing? Mary thought. She wondered what would have happened if he had looked hard enough and in the right place. The place she was trying so hard to find right now.

And then she heard the director say, "We're lucky that Biondi's front door's in such good condition. It's just what we need for the new wing of the museum."

Grandma's front door! Oh, no!

Mary closed her eyes. She leaned heavily against the ladder, which was as cold and damp and grimy as everything around her. What could she do?

"May I take away the door today?" Director Forrer was talking about the beautiful door to Grandma's house as though it were an old chair in a secondhand store.

"You may have it right now, sir." The supervisor's voice grew fainter as they moved away. "Come right along. I'll lift it off its hinges for you. I have my tools here." Mary heard the metallic *clank* as he slapped his pockets.

Anger surged up inside her, a frustrating, boiling fury. No, you won't give away my grandma's door! she thought.

Inside the black cavern of the stable she jumped from the middle rung of the ladder. Her foot slipped off the edge of a broken stone in the floor and plunged into what felt like soft, damp earth. It sank into the soggy mass, down, down.

She felt the suck at her ankle. Then, to her astonishment, her leg sank farther—almost to her knee!

Unbalanced by this abrupt pull, she heaved herself backward and sat down hard. Gasping, she planted both hands flat on the slippery stone beside her and yanked her leg up with all her strength.

Her leg was freed, but her boot—her boot was gone.

Below her she heard a crunching sound, either beams or plaster, a hollow *plop,* then a shower of fragments that sounded like broken stone, blobs of soil. She heard her boot land somewhere!

There was something below this hole in the stable floor! If only she could see! If only she could peer down that hole! If only she had a flashlight, a spade, an old sand shovel!

Those rooms—the secret room, the kiln room— could be down there!

On hands and knees she crawled away from the broken floor toward the stable door. Cobwebs did not bother her now, nor did the caked and musty burlap, lichen-crusted stone, piles of metal. She had to get out of this place. She had to stop those men!

She staggered up unevenly on one booted foot, the other wet and sticky with claylike mud, and

she fell against the door, plunging into the courtyard on her hands and knees.

"Stop!" she cried to the empty alley. Handi-
capped by the lost boot, she slipped and slid
toward the grimy door at the end. "Stop! Stop!
Stop!"

The narrow alley door was swinging open as
Mary, swaying unevenly, staggered past. But the
side lane was no longer empty. It was blocked
to the public by wooden sawhorses and red and
white signs reading in German: DANGER! NO
ENTRANCE!

A figure at the top of the lane waved wildly,
shouting, "Look out!" but Mary darted straight
toward him and the yellow truck behind him.

At the top of the lane, she swerved out of the
man's reach, slithered between the truck and
the corner house, ducked as she saw—too late—
the iron ball swinging out not far above her head.
It was aimed for the second story of the house.
She felt the *whoosh* lift the ribbons of her cap.

Bright blue eyes, red cheeks, tousled hair
blurred together. A hand came out of nowhere.
Paul yanked. And they fell in a heap, rolling well
past the house just as glass, wood, stone, and
metal crashed, tinkled, splintered, and cracked
behind them.

103

"I *thought* you'd be down here!" Paul gasped. "Told your family. They're coming—"

But Mary was not listening.

Untangling herself, completely unaware of the stunned witnesses behind them, of her mother, father, and Aunt Rosa running toward them across the square, she shouted to Paul, "Come on! We've got to stop them!"

On Grandma's steps she flung herself at the supervisor and pushed at the open door. "Don't do any more!" she yelled. "Don't take that door away! Please, *please!* Come with me!"

She was at the top of the corkscrew staircase before anyone could utter a sound.

14

Beyond the Wall

The next few moments were a jumble of shouts and stumbling in the dim hall and on the dark staircase.

Mary heard Paul behind her, the supervisor behind him. The light from his giant flashlight threw dancing shadows on the stairwell as he followed them down, protesting all the way.

Then, Oh! Thank goodness! Out of all the confusion she heard her mother and father! The glimpse of them as she and Paul had dashed into the house registered only then.

At the bottom of the stairs she flung back an arm, wriggled past Paul, and grasped her father's hand, her mother's hand.

"You're here! You've come just in time! Daddy, tell them," she pleaded breathlessly. "Tell them that a room could be boarded up!"

She dragged her father across the shadowy cellar to the wall. "Here," she insisted. "Right here!" She smacked her muddy mitten against the rough surface. "There's a room back there. *Two rooms!*"

She turned and glared up at the supervisor and Director Forrer.

"Oh, Daddy! Make them knock down that wall! Please! Please!" she cried.

In the glow from the flashlight six pairs of eyes, five grown-up men and women—and Paul—looked down at her.

When no one moved or answered her, not even her father, Paul stepped over to the supervisor.

In clear and positive Swiss German he said, "I think there could be a room back there. And I don't see why you won't knock down this wall. You're knocking down these houses, after all." His chin seemed squarer, his eyes brighter, his hair more stubborn than ever.

Mary did not feel like laughing at him anymore. No one laughed. Her father moved close to the wall, turned, said something to the supervisor. Miraculously hammer and chisel and other tools appeared. While Director Forrer held the flashlight steady, her father and the supervisor proceeded to tap the wall methodically.

A sudden hollow *thunk* stopped them. They glanced quickly at the director.

"Why not get some good tools now," Director Forrer said. "Why not"—he smiled at Mary, then at Paul—"stop work on the corner house and bring a few men over here?"

"Will—will—" Mary's voice barely carried across the basement to the supervisor, who was striding back toward the stairs. But he turned to listen. "Will they do it carefully?" she appealed to him. "The door's so beautiful."

"They'll do it carefully," he promised.

When the men started working, Mary stood well back from the wall within the circle of her mother and father's arms. She was happy and sad at the same time, if that could be possible. Deep inside her was the fear that this was the end of something precious, the belief that whether they found the room or not, she would never find Angelica again.

She flinched at the first shattering crack of plaster and stone. Then, before their eyes, the wall split open. One workman stepped back, turned to the supervisor. The other, more adventurous, thrust an arm all the way into the opening.

Over his shoulder he muttered, "Wood in there, sir. Carved, I'd say."

"Pull the plaster away," the supervisor said gruffly, "and be careful."

Mary's heart started to beat wildly while the men worked. It must be there! The room *must* be beyond that dark, jagged hole.

No one noticed that Paul had left Aunt Rosa's side and, on his knees, was pushing away fallen plaster and stone as fast as the workmen dropped it.

"Hey, look!" he yelled. He yanked out a shaft of iron a little longer than a half-used pencil topped by an upside-down heart.

"My key!" Mary leapt from her place between her mother and father and darted to Paul. Her fingers closed around the worn iron shaft once more. "Oh, *how* did it get—"

She did not finish the sentence, for a deep gasp came from everyone in the cellar.

The flashlight beamed through a wide opening, over a carved and paneled door set deeply in its recess.

Mary's breath caught in her throat.

It was the first time the door had been closed, the first time Angelica had not lighted the way.

Or had she lighted the way, always, all these

years for Grandma, and for Mary? Was she lighting the way now, for all of them?

It is up to me now, Mary thought. She held the key.

She stepped over the heaps of plaster and stone and inserted the key beneath the iron latch. The click, as the tumblers meshed with the old bit, was sharp in the silence.

Before the astonished gathering, the walnut door sighed open on its ancient hinges.

"Little one"—the supervisor's hand was on her shoulder—"you must let me go through first." He was polite but firm. "I must see whether it is safe or not."

As he bent his head to pass below the lintel, his torch flashed into the room beyond, into the secret room. Mary, with Paul beside her, was only inches behind him. All three stopped over the threshold.

Surrounded by mud, splintered timber, and broken stone, a rubber boot lay right in the middle of the tiled floor of the secret room.

There was no doubt how the boot had reached there. From a jagged hole in the ceiling, a small clod of mud gathered and dropped as they looked up.

Director Forrer, behind them now, spoke first. Crammed into the recessed doorway with her mother, father, Aunt Rosa, and the workmen, he said, "Rosa, I think your niece has found our lost treasures."

Across the room the edge of the flashlight's ray glinted on Anton Biondi's tile stove and the rippled roof of Angelica's pink doll's house.

Mary looked down then. She noticed that the Mary doll was missing from the doorstep. Of course—there had been no navy wool cut from the hem of her jumper. She had discovered this only when she had turned up the hem in Aunt Rosa's hall.

The Mary doll had simply disappeared, just as the spice cake and dark bread had.

When she stood still she felt her mother and father draw her close. With tears in her eyes, she saw the room as it had been during her afternoon with Angelica, warm and aromatic and glowing softly in the candlelight.

Except for the boot that lay there, the room looked just as though Angelica might have wandered off minutes ago. But to Mary it was cold and full of shadows, full of reminders. And worse than anything, no one was there to welcome them.

Still clutching the key, she moved a little away from the gathering behind her, unaware of the glances that followed her, especially Paul's. At

110

the table, which was as smooth as tile beneath her fingers, she stared at the smaller door, remembering the girl who had come to her with crisp cakes and warm milk.

She moved slowly toward the smaller door, touched it tentatively, and it creaked back a few inches, then stopped.

"Angelica . . ." Mary leaned forward into the darkness but almost immediately felt a hand light on her shoulder. She shook off the touch. "Angelica," she murmured, "are you there?"

Paul, behind her, grasped the collar of her coat. "There's no one there," he muttered. "Come back."

"Sh-h-h. Don't interrupt." Mary heard, if he did not, the whispered words that came from a faint glow in the darkness.

"Thank you, Mary." It was Angelica's voice, light as a summer breeze, and far away. *"Thank you—"*

The room beyond was totally dark again, and silent. Through her tears Mary managed to look up at her mother, who was closer than she had thought.

"There's more," was all Mary could say, "in there." She touched the door.

Director Forrer strode past her to the smaller door, and Mary was glad that he opened it with

111

care. She was not surprised that he stopped on the threshold, holding a borrowed flashlight.

"It's all here," he said finally, casting a grateful look at Mary. "Everything we've searched for is in these rooms. And more. The kiln—all of this belongs in a museum. Or, better still, this *house* could be the museum's annex."

It was Paul who broke the stunned silence. A series of exclamations burst from him, no doubt the Swiss equivalent of "Super! Cool! Great!" Then, edging over to Mary, he grinned at her. "That's what you wanted from the very first, wasn't it? You never wanted them to knock down these houses."

Mary ducked her head, embarrassed. With the toe of her booted foot, she maneuvered the muddy boot toward her. She might have lost a friend who had lived here, she thought. But, like Grandma, she had her memories.

And she had gained a new friend, she knew that now. Maybe many new friends.

15

Friends

From the wide window in Aunt Rosa's sitting room, Mary peered down at the picture-book scene of Wintertal. The exciting day was nearly over. It was suppertime, and dusk hung like a mist over the old town, dulling the brick-red roofs and pastel colors of the stone.

Grandma's house with its twin dormers and its single chimney stood proudly upright across from the cathedral just as it had for nearly four hundred years. Just as it would forever.

Mary sighed with happiness. So much had happened because of Grandma's dream, and Mary's dream, and the old key.

And now everyone was gathered in the room behind her to talk and explain and conjecture. After all, who really knew what happened four centuries ago? They could only guess from the history of the town.

Paul, who had been invited to supper, moved next to her. "Did you hear what that man said?"

"What man?" She was still thinking of the events of the day just past.

Paul groaned. "Don't tell me you're still dreaming. The *director,* of course."

"Oh, about my grandmother's house?"

"About those special rooms you found. Those two that were boarded up for nearly four hundred years."

"I heard most of it," Mary said.

"To think that you jumped off an old ladder and landed next to that trapdoor. Wow!"

"Trapdoor?" Mary blinked around at him. "I thought it was a loose stone in the stable's floor."

"You *weren't* listening," he accused.

Mary bit her lip. During the past half hour her mind had wandered once in a while. Now she tried to concentrate, to recall the details.

Paul helped. "You see, some people went underground when this town was sold to the canton capital in the sixteenth century."

114

"A canton is like a state, isn't it?" she asked then.

"Yes, and under its new ruler, it was *worse* than when the Austrians ruled it. People got angry about taxation without representation. The artist who owned the pink house—"

"That artist was Anton Biondi," Mary said. "I heard about what *he* did. And I think he was very smart to get that whole group of tile artists together and hide."

"They built two rooms to work in, at the end of the cellar."

"Beneath the stable," Mary murmured almost to herself. "That's why there weren't any windows."

"And," Paul went on, "they fitted every stone over that trapdoor so carefully that it looked just like one flat floor in the stable. No one suspected it was there."

In a flash Mary recalled the swift glance Angelica had sent toward the ceiling that first day. She nodded.

"Then they carried out their tiles as they baked them and built their stoves as far away as they could get."

Mary thought of Angelica waiting for her father to return while she wove his cloth and baked his bread. And dressed the dolls for the little

115

house, which Director Forrer said was priceless. She was afraid to look at Paul for fear the tears in her eyes would betray her. She looked away, down the hill.

Lights were going on, one by one, in the old town now. Someday soon Grandma's house would be lighted again. Mary leaned her forehead against the cold pane of the window.

Paul looked out, too. "Did you hear what they're going to do about those houses?"

"You mean my grandmother's house, the Biondi house? It's going to be a museum, isn't it?"

"All the houses." There was a note of respect in his voice. "They're even going to restore the one they started to knock down."

"I'm glad," Mary said. "Then they'll all look right, as though they belonged together, just like the artists who lived there and worked together so long ago. There'll be no funny-looking glass and—and—"

"Concrete." Paul supplied the word she was searching for. "That's what they build with now." He hesitated briefly. "I suppose they *could* put that new town building up on the hill somewhere."

"I'm sure they can," Mary said. "There's plenty of room."

116

After a moment Paul said, "You're funny," and Mary felt him glance at her.

The pause before she spoke was longer. "Why?" she asked finally.

"Not funny, exactly." It was another moment before he added, "Different. In fact," he went on, "you're the most *different* girl I've ever known." He kicked the fringe on the rug. "I—uh—hope it snows when you come back from your trip to the Engadine with your mother and father. We can go up to the big hill then."

"I hope it snows, too," Mary said.

About the Author

RUTH WILLOCK has written many romantic suspense novels and short stories for adults, including *The Night of the Visitor* and *The Street of the Small Steps*. This is her first novel for young readers. When she is not in Zürich, she resides in New York City.